SOULSHIP

SOULSHIP

*Love letters between
distant lovers*

HUMA & RIVER

To Love and Heartbreak.
Without you, I would have never learned life's deepest
lessons.
- Huma

To everyone
who told me a "no"
So that I could learn
to tell myself a thousand "yes"
- River

Praise for Soulship

"Initially, when you start reading, you wonder how love could be so sudden, verbose, excessive, and romantic to the point of madness. It is ridiculous... But then you remember being in the same exact point of mania, and you know, you spoke of forevers too, said always, said until the last star burns out, like love would never end until it did and even then, it lived on."

- Danabelle Gutierrez
UAE based writer, actress and photographer

Praise for Soulship

"Introducing Huma and River, the brilliant authors behind the captivating letter series - *Soulship* that unfolds the intricacies of love, distance, and self-discovery. With a unique narrative style, they delve into the complexities of relationships, exploring the depths of emotions through a series of heartfelt letters. their words resonate with wisdom, vulnerability, and a profound understanding of the human experience.

Huma not only an author but also a cherished friend, brings a refreshing perspective on love and connection. Her letters are a testament to the power of introspection, recognizing the diverse facets of love, and the journey towards self-realization. Through the pages of her book, readers embark on a transformative voyage, navigating the ebbs and flows of relationships and uncovering the richness of the human heart.

A storyteller with a keen insight into the human soul, Huma weaves a narrative that transcends the conventional boundaries of love and separation. Her exploration of the self, wrapped in the guise of letters, adds a layer of authenticity and relatability to her work. Readers are invited into a world where every emotion is laid bare, every struggle is acknowledged, and every lesson is embraced with gratitude.

Huma's *Soulship* is not just a collection of letters; it's a profound exploration of the tapestry of human connections, making her a distinctive voice in contemporary literature. As a dear friend, her warmth, wisdom, and genuine spirit shine through both in her writing and in the bonds she fosters. Huma's literary journey is an invitation to reflect, connect, and appreciate the beauty found within the intricacies of the heart."

- Mohammed Abrar Ahmed

Author of *Daydreams and Midnight Realities* and *Petrichor*

Soulship

My Dearest Friend (if that's what I shall call you),

Today is the fourth day since we met, and the fire we made in the forest on the first day is still burning. The memories we created in the woods have ignited my soul. The words uttered from your lips have swirled my soul, and I am no longer myself. I am not YOU yet. But I know there is a wind blowing around me, asking for unfamiliar lands and an unknown destiny. Do not worry; the feet are not afraid of uneven paths. They aren't even scared of wet floors. If to fall is a fate, I would fly.

We should not think of the dark days that haven't approached yet. I must take your soul to the day when we began our journey; the day when my heart refused to be in its territory and turned against me. It has never been my ally, and the day it saw you, it proved to be truer than ever.

Now, as we have become more than acquaintances, I wonder what name I shall give you. Should it be a friend, or shall I elevate you to soulmate? I tried to look deeper into this thought and realized that you are a traveler. Not a hermit or nomad, but rather a business-class traveler who lets his body travel through means of luxury. While I am a nomad; class haunts me, and mud appeals to me. While you sit in theaters and applaud the world's known artists, I, on the other hand, praise art lying under the skies and among the mountains.

You fill your fingertips by touching delicate skins; I let mine burn day and night. And yet, you are as empty as I am.

Do you think we shall fill our souls and feed our starving hearts? Do you think we would be able to heal our bodies without ever owning each other?

I must wait for your answer, and till then, I shall call my heart home. You see, it's getting darker out there, and this little troublesome piece is not willing to give up hope of finding light once again.

You stay as you are, magical and warm.

Yours (if I am one),

Whosoever

My dear, whose name fills my mouth syllable after syllable until it's flooded with a taste sweeter than honey, is my favorite unit of measurement to count the time. The said time is now my enemy. I cannot hear it mentioned or referred to without thinking about the past, in which you and I were closer; about the present, for whose cruel decree we're currently afar; and about the future, still too foggy and undecipherable, concerning our fate.

My eyes divert, like in front of a horrible monster, whenever I see the current time being shown, and I admit it happens so often that if I adjusted and bore its existence and display, then my time (argh!) would feel way less miserable. But I can't prevent the world from showing hours, minutes, and seconds! What is this obsession we have with time?

Perhaps, do we think that by counting it, by showing how much we treasure it, we might gain some? How foolish! On the contrary, to count it is rather to waste it! Or perhaps, this is a warning about death ready to fall on us and crush us one of these days? Ah, what a pleasant way to live, with that anguish constantly before our eyes! Again, shouldn't we use our precious time to do something better than checking its run? To live, for example! And let's be honest: slow or fast, that final day will come for each one of us, anyway. (Not for you. No. I simply refuse to consider the idea.)

Oh, they may even obsess us with this time and its crazy run... but in my home, at least, I can choose to ignore it! At first, I removed the batteries from the wall clocks (their ticks and tocks were simply unbearable!). I set them at the time in which we last said goodbye (a temporary one: I can't accept any other way); but it was too saddening. Then I soon changed it to a time in which we were happy; but it felt so wrong and painful, without you by my side. So I simply turned the clocks towards the wall, to not read them anymore.

But then I thought of all the things that still remind me of the passage of time (without you). From the plants on the balcony growing, blossoming, and withering; to the food in the fridge getting stale and stinky. When I noticed that even my heart, with its unstoppable beat, keeps reminding me of the continuous fall and accumulation of layers of time, I had to surrender and declare my defeat: it can neither be stopped nor ignored.

And then I found the key to accepting all this: rather than counting time from the last moment when my arms wrapped around your body and I inhaled that flowery smell of your hair... I can count down to the moment, somewhere in the future when we will meet again. But then I wonder: where should I start it from, that blessed countdown? As you can see, time is not really my friend when it comes to you. How do you deal with it?

Oh, how I cherish our time together! Feels like a dream. I'm yours, always and forever.

P.S. 1 I wouldn't want you to be anyone but the very you. I could not take it any other way! If you weren't you, see, any law could break, and the universe would fall apart. That's why I disagree on the statement that you (and I) are empty. Tell me, how can a creature being described as 'empty' feel like a universe of possibilities? My soul would grow old while exploring it and could never finish this task. Each one of us is more complex than that dimensionless point the Big Bang used to be before starting space and time, I believe! Your future, no less, comes into reality from your existence.

P.S. 2 "Theaters?" "Luxury?" Oh, dear, no. Just, no. When you'll know me better, you'll realize. My imagination provides me with the most adventurous journeys, from where the rings of Saturn are just a remote and fading memory, to the farthest place: that in which I do the things I'm scared of doing.

P.S. 3 Oh, that forest! The trees, and their shadows, seemed to dance before our eyes, to celebrate our happiness!

My dearest and my very own,

I received your letter, and I couldn't stop myself from reading and rereading it. You talk of distance, and I felt none as I was under the spell of your words. Do not fear time, my love. It is the most important yet the cruelest invention of man. What the heart holds, needles can never. Trees might lose their leaves. The milk can go bad. The colors would fade. What stays constant is my love. Your love. Our love.

You are my muse, my song, my verse! When songs do not stop to amaze us even years and years later, then what is time to us? All I wonder is if I ever will be able to confess my heartstrings to you before our skin disappears, and bones become visible? But does a confession from the lips matter when the heart and soul are aware of our state? You are miles and miles away from me, but every morning when I wake up, I find the fragrance of Bvlgari blended with the odor of Jack Daniels on me. Isn't this an indication that we meet when the whole world falls asleep? But then again, when Asia sleeps, Europe is wide awake. How do we meet then?

But we are no ordinary beings. And as Faiz says, 'There are more pleasures than the pleasure of union.' Our union isn't of the body, but of the heart and soul. I hope we will see them united again one day. Your arms around me and my lips caressing yours.

When I was reading your letter, I came across the most beautiful pronoun which the English language has offered us, 'we.' I couldn't help but smile and cry. I smiled because I saw the tint of love on your heart. I cried because I feel I am unworthy of such honor. This very 'we' reminds me of Rumi,

"Someone asked, 'What is love?' I answered, 'You will know when you become 'we.'"

So 'we' has been an omen for centuries just like our souls who have met somewhere millions of years ago. Don't worry. Time doesn't scare me, and I know nor does it do you. Had it been anyone who should fear, it has to be the world. Because when the fire of two hearts spread, it doesn't burn one or two. It turns the whole world into ashes.

Light the torch and set the fire!

Yours, Forever.

My dear,

If you were unworthy, if you really thought that, then you should come to the conclusion to doubt and contest my judgment (other than yourself) when I say and proclaim you're a true gem among the human kind. Would you be ready to do that?

I'm not saying your worth is either given or sanctified or legitimized by my appreciation and adoration of you. Not at all. Your worth... well, tell me that a creature able to love, like you are and do, isn't worthy, if you can! And tell me that a creature able to so gracefully express such an amount of love through her words, like you beautifully do, isn't worthy, if you can!

I'm just saying you need no validation from anyone, not even from me. So I won't limit myself to say that you, body and soul, have been able to move and attract me, body and soul, like a wildly burning giant star would attract some planets to be perpetually and willingly linked, bound, chained around itself. I will say that such a burning star would still be and still is bright, warm, powerful, and generous even without planets dancing around it. That burning star could still be able to make possible warmth, light, life, somewhere in an otherwise cold, dark, and dead area in the vast universe.

Moreover, if you really think you're not worthy, would you send me away? Because if you love me (and I'm sure you do), then you have to want the best for me. Please, never take such a route. It only leads to the destruction of all good things. Destruction... our bones, our skin... the thought of the world after us, going on as if we and our feelings never mattered, made me shed a tear!

Will they find these letters? Will they cry? Will they laugh? Will they consider such words empty? How will they understand it, the wish I have, at times, to grow taller than trees, taller than mountains, taller than the Earth! And to turn into a giant, with my big fingertips, to pinch the portion of Earth's crust between us so to make our places get closer and... oh, what am I saying?! We would get a mountain, or a chain of mountains then between us, and this already low chance to meet and being close, once again, would get even lower!

How will they understand, that impression to be walking barefoot on scorching stones, or on shards of perennial eyes, or to wish to open my ribcage to check why my heart seems not to beat anymore for your absence? Yet, they love. We love. We have always been. So, they will understand, I guess, at least within the limits of their own experience.

Ah, my dear, I don't want you to suffer! I look at myself in the mirror and I invite myself to 'Look within! Deeper and deeper!' Bodies will perish, you got it right. Yet souls, energy, and love, will remain. I believe our souls never got separated, since they looked out from the windows that are our eyes and saw each other and formed that hug they've been certainly sharing. And what if they had been hugging each other even from before that moment?! They need no words, souls. Neither inked nor pronounced. It's my belief, that spiritual hug. It's my life's buoy, in this stormy sea of distance in which even the waves stay away from each other, but then all collapse on us, I don't know whether to torture us or to caress us.

Yours. That's what I am. "Mine", that's how you could call me.

P.S. How sweet! How peculiar! There would be no "we"

without "I" and "I". Look at that "W"! What do you see? I see two I-s, at the sides, both almost losing their senses for the immense joy of being together, yet standing up, together, joined by their hands!

–Mine! Yes, All Mine!

What a pleasure it is to call you mine, and now when you have given me all the rights, then why must I not take a privilege and make you all mine? Now tell me, how are you, my heart? I hope your heart is as splendid as the spring of Eden. It's as cheerful as summer has never set its footsteps there. For you deserve the blooms that will surround you with the most darling odor for eternity.

Do you even know what you are to me? All those stars you talk about, if gathered and burned on one sky, wouldn't suffice to display the love my small red organ holds. Since the day I have chosen to love you, my heart has grown, and sometimes it seems to me that my body is shrinking or the expansion of the former is so much that I now live inside this humongous red house. But this love is a sweet poison. I know I am going to die without you, and I know I have to live for you. What shall I choose, my love?

I have chosen to call you Odin. Why? Well, your previous letter took me to a state from where coming back became not only difficult but almost impossible. I am not sure if I ever wanted to come, but hope isn't a good ally of mine. Hopelessness surrounded me, and I climbed the stairs down, leaving behind all the hope that I can be loved too, which was received from you.

You say I can move planets and stars for who I am, but you know what I care for? A place in your heart. Have you ever wondered what will become of our bodies if we die while being miles away? How much the idea of being buried away from you torments me? How can I ever embrace death without holding your hand?

Last night, I dreamt of riding with you into the woods where we met. Do dreams come true? If not in this world, then will you take me away in the other? Your saying that our souls are cuddling each other since eternity brought to my heart an unexpected pleasure. I am not used to such affection, but I shall treasure these words my entire life - a life that is to be spent without you.

I took your advice soberly, and it has made the thorns easy to walk over. However, I must confess, my mind is volatile like Mount Pinatubo, which erupted without any warning. But I don't fear that I might end up burning our mansion, for I have faith that on such occasions, you will warm me in your arms and let me be there until I am in my best senses.

Now when you desire me, I must bring this reality to you that I am not a voluptuous being, nor do I have such anatomy. Would I still be admirable to you? If so, then love me. Cosset me. Save me from me. And here I leave you with the shards of my heart and this,

"Is it too late to touch you, dear?"
We this moment knew –
Love marine and Love terrene –
Love celestial too –
Yours,
Well—
I am only Yours.

After so long since your last letter, I want my first words to you to be a heartfelt apology. I've been traveling, that's true, between the blue of the mirror and the gray falling of the hourglass, between the wooden roofs with hanging fans and the untamable concrete ruined by the indolence of men... but I could have verged down notes for my reply to you.

I apologize to you, for your sweet words and your adamant affection would have deserved a prompt reply. Why didn't I do it? Why didn't I write to you before? Not because I don't care: I implore you on my knees, never ever think that! To believe that would compare to thinking that the rain rises, rather than falling, from the ground to the sky!

But something, something in your words... scared me, I think. Oh, no, not your feelings for me! How could I be scared by such wholehearted surrendering?! It's sweet, and it makes me desire to lean on you, lift from the ground your delicate bones, and to bring you with me, in light flight, above the clouds and rest there, and look down at the people, and wonder which their thoughts and dreams are.

But there's rather something else, here and there, whose simple contemplation was simply impossible for me to bear. "I am going to die without you and I know I have to live for you. What shall I choose, my love?" This. This brought needles under my skin and a devouring emptiness in my heart and a dismaying sense of precipitating forever.

"Choose?" Is there really a choice here, my dear? You cannot die, even if, for now, you are without me. What is "without?" Physically, perhaps. But, look. I am yours. And you are mine, yes, mine. Can you really say that you are without me? If I were dead, then you could probably say that you would be without me, even though you could still reasonably suspect (for a reason) that my soul would still consider yours its privileged mate for an eternity.

If I ended up losing my mind, and I suddenly told you there's nothing more I want to do with you, then you could say you would be without me, in every way, not just the body, but heart, mind, and soul, as well. I can't caress your face whenever I want. But I can still trust that a light breath of wind will do it in my place, somehow, if I wish it strongly enough (and I do it, trust me).

I can't tell you, mouth to ear, how much I long for you. But you might, at any time, read such a line in a book, or watch an actor pronounce it in a movie, or hear someone say it referred to someone else... and then you could stay reassured that it would be the universe, in that moment, to say it to you on my behalf.

"...buried without you... embrace death..." Ah, this one, too! Why, why all these thoughts of death, now?! With which purpose? Life is our best ally, having it already planned each one's existence and then given us this chance to meet and lay each one's own heart in the others' chest!

Life is our best ally, offering to both of us that time in whose instants everything before unimaginable can finally turn in our favor! Death? If one of us left this world, how terrible it would be for the other to stay and survive and move on? Do you miss me, terribly? Do I miss you, terribly? Yes, and yes! But then, at least you exist, are alive and love me. But then, at least I exist, am alive and love you.

This is what life has currently to offer to us. Tell me now, what does death offer? Nothing good, for this bond we've been nurturing like a child. So, the way it is, is still much better than many other ways could be. Oh, my sweet Mount Pinatubo! I'll be the forest re-growing on your sides still exhaling feeble vapors, on the fertile ground of your apprehension first erupted and then cooling down, and my hug of tender and fresh lymph will soothe your fears.

"You will be sea, And I will be stone, sinking in you to find comfort and peace, Raising your waters in a joyful spurt, Till we will flood the sky And we will touch the moon Together" We are two, wherever we are. That's so much, if we think about it. May the earth turn to grass, and the stone to cloud, at your dear passage.

My mind contemplates your existence, and to my heart, you couldn't be closer, wherever you are, my dear you.

Yours,

"mine".

P.S. Odin? Oh, that's powerful! And lovely. I'll call you my Gaea, then. The place that wouldn't exist without the creative love of God. The place on which the praises of God are sung.

My Dearest,

I have been away. I have been here but away from my soul and heart. I was on a roller coaster of meeting and losing people. I am in utter pain. I feel the world around me is a mirage and with one touch it will disappear like a bubble. You do love me, but I know it's for today because tomorrow is uncertain. Humans are uncertain. One moment they choose you as their companion, and the next, they are just not sure.

I have bid so many farewells that now when a moment of parting comes, it seems déjà vu. It looks so familiar that now the word eternity sounds alien to me. I recently lost a friend I loved. Not to death, but to life. Perhaps that makes the pain harder to bear. This friend I am talking about came into my life to heal himself. He needed light, and when he had enough, he walked away saying he hates emotional attachment. Here, I am baffled, angry, and remorseful about trusting a human. The fact that I am a human too stabs my heart.

I don't want to die. I want to live, but more than wanting to live, I want people to live. I want love to live, but it seems God is failing me. God is hurting me. I am protesting against Him for taking away all that I love. My protest is not a hunger strike but to prevent myself from asking for more.

My sincerest apology for writing you such a sad letter. It's just that I am very sad. I am drowning in an ocean of sadness. I'm sorry for being so selfish that I forgot to ask about you. How are you, my love? The sad news is, stones are still stones, and the ground is still the ground. Nothing greener on my side.

Thank you for calling me Gaea. It's good to be called with a special name and to be assured we are loved.

Yours,
Sad Beloved.

Oh, you, sweet heart whose extension surpasses that of the universe!

How is it that those who love the most get left behind the most? Perhaps it's just a false perception: we all get left behind, but those who live the most, they also suffer the most. I have to admit that your letter drowned me in two kinds of storming seas of pain, whose chart of pain I couldn't determine.

First of all, the idea of you suffering so much: I know the extent to which you can love, the candour, like that of a child... I know, for you did it with me in the short amount of time we could spend together, how you can elect your beloved ones as your universe. My goodness, losing someone, in your candid eyes, probably feels like watching a portion of the stars suddenly falling from their place in the canvas down below the horizon destined to be lost! But then, dearest being under the sky, you say it already happened and many times! Why do you let it hurt you, every single time, as if it was the last one? Why do you still caress all those lambs, as if your hand wasn't already covered with scars, as if you didn't know that some of them might be ferocious wolves disguising themselves? Why do you expose your heart to those dangers, every time? Don't you know, that's your little lamb to protect? How can we blame God if we don't want to learn? You can learn, of course: your intelligence can make you treasure all the experience so far... you owe it to yourself, for it's an experience you accumulated at a very high price. You lost a false friend: how can this be bad? You really have yourself, and only yourself. Like I have myself... only myself? Do I have you? It's been a pain to read you doubt of me. What if I was one of those who stay? There's no promise able to grant anything, now. Only facts will tell. I know why you now doubt of me: you want to protect yourself from any other possible. But know you make it hard for me... and even more for yourself. You draw me towards yourself with one hand, and at once push me away with the other: if you don't trust the help you invoke, don't you see its beneficial effect will be nullified? At first, reading your heart-crushing letter, I wished you could say that you need me and only me: but that would be selfish. Of course, you need and deserve friends to surround you! I'm far away, but you're not alone. My prayers to God, His protection on you, can do for you more than an army could.

Stay blessed,
Light of my reason.

My Darling,

Don't think I don't love you. Don't think I am gone. I was just healing like that tree which sheds and grows its leaves back once the autumn is over. I do not say I have grown my leaves, but I think my branches are stronger. I am slowly trying to see the sun with my naked eyes. Perhaps, how long can I wear shades and avoid what is destined to happen?

My love, I can't love just one person. I feel my heart is that barrel of wine that doesn't serve just one! How can I love just one and let the whole world out of my sight? I, a perfect human body, was not created by God to just make love and pick petals to prophesize if I am loved or not.

Losing people I loved has taught me one thing: we all are born to do something, something to make this world a better place, yet some choose evilness over good. I, hereby, choose you but not you alone. I want to plant trees in a world which is on the urge of breaking apart. I want to be the light of someone's life! But, as much as I want to give, I desire to be loved! But my skin, which is too thick, comes in between my desire and you, and urges me not to beg for love, rather to take it as an honor bestowed upon me. What is the use of a love that has to be asked for?

Love should be rained upon us! Love must come on our way unasked and untimely.

I am not pushing you away! I want you as much today as I wanted yesterday, but to love me is no easy task. To love me is as if moving the mountains from land into the sea.

I love you, but what do I do with this heart who wants to love everything existing in this universe? I am sending you the warmth of my arms and heart!

Yours,
Yes, I am still Yours.

My dear!

What a relief, to read your latest letter. Relief for myself and for you. It was like opening a window on a sunny sky in a room suffocated by darkness. Oh, how could I ever want to be the only one in your life? It would be selfish, twice (at least)! For I cannot fool myself into believing I could ever give you all the love you need and deserve. I'm a person with flaws, limits, weaknesses... there might be circumstances in which I could not provide you, despite my best intentions and efforts, with the kind of love, help, or support you might exactly need.

An athlete might take you on their shoulders and let you cover a certain distance as quickly as possible. But if you had to solve a spiritual problem, would such a person be the best choice, advice-like? Who knows! An aged guru, on the other hand, would easily not be the best choice if you needed someone provided with physical strength, but would certainly fit if you needed someone's advice. And a child? Or even someone childish. Wouldn't such a person remember and teach you how to play, and let your inner child smile? You never know, which kind of friend you might need, somewhere in time.

You would deserve to be surrounded by many, many friends, and be hugged, smiled at, cherished, and helped at any moment... I could erase this last line, but I won't. Because I want this to be like a conversation, and we know we can't take back our words, once we pronounced them, no matter what. I want you to have friends taking care of you, yes... but not too many, not to the point of you forgetting how beautiful it is to be with your own company, how beautiful it is to take care of yourself and realize that you can do it.

And as I told you, I would never want the world to have to renounce all the light you can shower it with... it would be too selfish on my side! There is too much darkness that can be wiped away or at least weakened by the light you so spontaneously and generously radiate. It just takes for you to remember and never forget that you're light yourself, and nurture that which you produce within.

I remember my last letter to you... and now, your words: love is not supposed to be begged for, to be asked for... as if it was a right, I add. And I realize how much I sounded like a beggar, crying and sobbing, at the idea of your love suddenly seeming lost... as if, like you in that letter, whom I was pretending to enlighten and lead, I was reacting to the apparent loss of you, exactly like you were reacting to your friend's loss.

Are we clay giants, in truth, whose gargantuan feet can be shaken and abated by a wind which is forceful enough? I feared to lose you, and in the process, I was losing myself. Do I even know I live, I exist, and I have bones to support myself, muscles and nerves to lead my steps somewhere, and one heart, one mind, one soul, to decide where that "somewhere" is?

I was here begging you to give me love, as if I was a beggar who doesn't know how to be rich. Or a beggar who could be rich if he wasn't also a thief who was stealing from himself. But I am rich with love; I finally have to admit it. How could I find any, in myself, to freely offer to you, otherwise? Indeed, I find plenty of it within, of that love for you.

Thank you, my teacher and my heart. Even your desperation is generous of lessons. But I hope, pray, and wish with all of myself that you might always be in peace and overflowing happiness.

Yours,

"Mine"

My Dearest and Precious,

I woke up today smiling after a long time. I don't remember the last time when my day started with hope. I don't remember the last time I felt my existence. Today, I felt you next to me. Close to me. So close that I could hear the sound of our heartbeats entwining and dancing, producing the most beautiful rhythm. The patch of light coming through the window and first touching your face and then mine is enough to glow my entire life.

I am somewhere between existence and death. I want you as much as I want to fly! Yes, I do love you, but seeing love can take away the rosy cheeks, the ocean of the heart, and the tickling in the gut scares me. I want my heart to always jump when I see you! But every day brings love in a different frequency. Every day, I grab a coffee from the same place, yet every day I complain it doesn't taste as on day one. Because every moment, every emotion, and every heartbeat is unique. It cannot be ever produced with the same effect again.

I want you, but I don't want you to get used to me so much that your heart stops bothering you when I am around. I want it to always make you jump! To glow! To smile! I don't want to fall from the ladder where you have elevated me.

Do you know I suffer from darkness? I fight my demons all night and wake up with swollen eyes. But since the world around me is so used to the masquerade I play, I have to put on a mask and give a performance of happiness, of joy, and pretend all is well when it isn't.

To keep the curtains pulled, I might not be ever able to unite my body with yours. I might never have a union of fingers, arms, and lips with you. But I give you my soul, love.

None of the holy books have oaths written for lovers like us. I am writing ours! Go to the beach, look at the sea, pick the shell, and read this oath. Drop the shell into the ocean. I would do the same, so our souls will travel the seas together till we are destined for the worldly knot.

"Oh the Lord of the ocean, the sea, this shell, and our souls, in Thy name I choose to love my soulmate. In Thy name, I promise to love this person till I am risen again on the resurrection day and united physically. Oh my Lord! Make this love purer than the water of heaven's fountains. Make our hearts filled with love as Thy fill Eden with beauty! My Lord! Unite our spirits for the sake of Thy love! I promise I shall continue to love and care for her/him despite distance, heartbreak, and hardships. Let this shell travel and meet the shell carrying my beloved's soul. Make us one when you choose to, till then let our souls love and grow."

You are mine in the world hereafter.

Yours!

Only Yours!

My Love,

I will. I will. I will. I will collect a shell, one I will rationally believe I picked randomly amongst a thousand, but rather whose specimen, material, shape, colors, smell, inhabitants, travels together with its unique name will have been recorded in that catalog of everything, the immense book of the universes, written by God Himself. In the same moment the Big Bang happened and everything was, and your existence, and mine, were decided and considered unavoidable and precious by nothing less than human decree. This will break the dams of my soul, and tears will fall on the shell and will fill it with water as saline as that of the sea. And the sea will be at once mother and daughter, and in the singularity of my existence, past and present will balance each other, and time won't make any sense anymore, and the secret of eternity will be revealed. The thought that you enclose and embed the same infinity will make a smile blossom through my tears as if it were a white flower in soil soaked with life.

I will collect a shell, and I will shrink myself to the size of a breath whispering the words "I love you." I will venture into its spiraling cavities, turning and turning and turning and turning until I reach its fractal center. Here where they say a word takes birth from the sacred love between a thought and a feeling, the mind and the heart finally at peace and in perfect harmony with each other. A lifetime, and all the lifetimes, breathing, laughing, and singing at once, in a humongous concert of tribute to the beauty of life, to the stupor for the gift of existence, and all that is beautiful which can follow it. In such a loud symphony, through the moving noise of uncontainable joy, I'll still be able to hear the whisper coming from the heart of the sea, and it will tell your name, because that has been the shell I picked on your sacred command, and it couldn't be any other way.

And I will collect one more shell, ten, one hundred, one thousand, one million, one billion, one trillion more shells. I will raze the oceans with all its remains of life which once used to be and now they're no more, and I will pile it all – shells, bones, teeth, and I will erect a lighthouse to climb so I can look at you from a distance and with a gargantuan iceberg bend the rays of the sun to silently send you messages from my inner universe. I will turn the tower into a minaret to call you to the prayer to the God who can do everything for us if we believe it hard enough, and if we pray hard enough. If it's in His undecipherable will and plan, I will turn the minaret into a bell tower, from which I will ring all the bells. I will steal from Heaven, and all the angels will start imploring God to make it happen, no matter what He had planned. This impossible union, to turn this distance into the most intersecting closeness, to the point of making us like one being, one soul, one mind, one heart, one flesh, one bone, one blood, one marrow, just like one added to one can equal one if only God wants it.

Days are changing, time is unrolling, nothing is like before, before is like nothing, and tomorrow is unknown. Yet the equation is always marvelously fulfilled, written by God, the greatest mathematician and physician. No matter how many variables might change, on both the sides of such equation, you and I, as terms, as ever-evolving constants, will be always there, producing from within all the changes each one of us will need to stay the most true to oneself, and all the other terms will simply adapt to that. And the equality sign in between – balancing the mother and the daughter – balance which supports and grants anything and everything that is our love, which will always be true.

I will. I will. I will.

I, and my will, are all I have, are all I am. I am, therefore I love. And you are, therefore I love, and I feel I am more myself because I love the shells, the towers, the saltwater, the angels, God.

You.

With these vows, we become one! In the name of Love, love bestowed upon us by yours and my Lord, we are inseparable now.

Being miles and miles away, I can feel your soft lips on my fingertips. I can feel the warmth of your body over mine. I can hear your breath every morning when the sun touches me. It kisses my eyes and whispers, "From your beloved." I ask it, if the God of Heaven and Earth will forgive me for falling in love with a man who speaks a different language, practices a religion which has a different holy book than mine, and lives in culture whose colors, food, and music are alien to me. The sun says it is for you to ask God not it. So I wrote to God. He said I can listen to my heart and I can love what I choose to love but to love Him more. Since it is He who holds my soul, and loves me more than 70 mothers.

My Beloved, God didn't tell me if I can ever have you, but I can love you. I might not ever wake up to the day when the sun would touch our bodies together, but I promise you that you will always wake up to find me right in your heart. I want to steal you, but what shall I do about the manmade borders – a small piece of paper deciding where we can or cannot travel? How shall I steal you from those who dearly love you? All I can do is accept this unfathomable mathematics of the universe. All that is in my power is just to love you! Will I ever be the one who would sing to you before bedtime? Will I ever be the one who would kiss away the drops of wine from your lips? Will I ever be the one to put my arms around you while you will be breaking down? Will I ever be the one to make coffee while you hug me and place your lips on my neck? Will I ever be the one to hold your hand and walk into a garden that would witness our love for thirty years? Am I asking too much from life? Am I desiring the forbidden apple? Even Adam and Eve found their way back to each other, will we?

It was Christmas when I had a small wish to have you as my friend. Here is another Christmas when I have you as my lover. I fear what next Christmas will bring. Will it bring 'us' or 'you and I'? Tell Santa that I am not Christian, but when it comes to giving, Santa doesn't care what religion the receiver belongs to.

I do wonder if our bodies are destined to unite in this world or not. However, I am not worried about our hearts. They are already united for eternity.

Yours,

Beloved.

I miss you.

I wish I could peel off my skin like an orange-coated moon because my skin craves to be melted in the boiling, burning, magmatic, nuclear heat of the saliva left by your kisses. It cries unintelligible prayers from each pore like a mouth wide open before I prudently remind it that you can't be here, and then ranting laments of despair after I've done it.

I wish I could remove it - origin after origin, detaching them like when you dismantle a complex gizmo and put aside the pieces in an ordered and sorted fashion so to be able to at least try to put it together later, belly after belly, insertion after insertion, the throbbing masses of the muscles that contract in the tension which is so natural after the daydream of hugging you tight. My muscles relax, but no, they don't; they just get exhausted at the idea of the previous effort that counted for nothing. And yet they believe that perhaps, by contracting themselves tighter and tighter, you and your body will be next to mine... and tell me what I could do, if not wishing to detach them from my skeleton, if they destroy themselves in this energetic effort which doesn't shorten our inacceptable distance?

I wish I could disarticulate my skeleton, bone after bone, and compose it into a new form. An impossible creature nowhere to be found in the books of paleontology, zoology, biology, or even in the imaginary bestiaries that imaginative men with not enough dust under their feet but enough fantasy in their heads used to compose. And when I had done so, when such an impossible creature, the most wondrous ever seen, necessarily had gained life, I could let it crawl, walk, hop, fly from all these things together, away, away from me.

I wish I could cover, walk, sink, and detach my eyes, for

they make me look for your eyes darker than the night behind every sunny corner. My nose, for it voluptuously inhales volumes of air sufficient to wrap a blue whale, in search of the rose-scented smell of your hair. My ears, for it filters your voice, your whispers, your laughter, in the cacophonies rising from any crowd, any sea, any flock of birds chirping in the trees.

I wish I could deprive myself of anything material, concrete, heavy, warm, pulsating, and compose this shattered being I have become through the years, or the years have made me become, or on which I have patched the years like a tailor gone insane, of anything material – I was saying – which, for the most mysterious yet predictable laws of alchemy, can only crave what has kinship with it: your body. And it's my body as well. The responsible for my perennial, inextinguishable pain, ache, torment, for it needs to sense, touch, squeeze, weigh, measure, for that is its language, its dictionary, its grammar, like a clouded servant unconsciously referring and getting messages only the master, an ancient scholar who grew old and stayed young by studying the infinities, can properly compose and decipher.

The pain of this unbearable distance, the ache of this world of people like us who seem to rejoice in putting obstacles, barriers, difficulties, challenges, prohibitions between us, as if they wanted to deny us what they couldn't even dare to dream to have. All this wall of many little bricks grotesquely provided with mouths first saying their countless "no!" to us and then sarcastically laughing at our face, and spitting on our feelings, all this would be gone and forgotten. If there wasn't the body, if there wasn't the world, if there wasn't matter, if we were left in the perfect state of souls, floating in everything, everywhere, forever. God is not needing to fill anything with anything, for being already the dimensionless and timeless concept of existence. Unlike we do by always filling everything, because of our natural condition of lacking something, someone, somewhere, sometime for the limits inscribed in our bodies.

Christmas!

That's the paradox I love the most!

The divine love embracing the human misery, for to save it from the outside, for to comfortably sit on a throne away from the pain of the world just wasn't enough. And we feel like shrinking back to the state of children, with so many days ahead that they seem infinite. And we make wishes as if a whole life hadn't been consumed in dreams, we weren't able to prevent from shattering in our own shaking hands.

On Christmas, as if only on that day it was possible to find that innocence which has always been within our heart, and we always suffocated under a stinking mass of sins we ravenously let sink in our skin for to let them stain our soul so to proudly define ourselves adults. But on Christmas day, we can believe we can be made anew, as if nothing happened, or better, as if everything happened but everything had been forgotten and forgiven as well.

And we don't know, in our physical obsession for measuring and weighing, that we don't need to wait another year to fill our hearts bursting with confetti of hope and joy, that we don't need to drag ourselves throughout a year of shadows to see that one day of light, suddenly followed by the sunset of the joy vanishing too soon. We don't know that our soul is a burning fire which knows no weakness, no extinction, no thirst for fueling gratifications, no hunger for feeding dreams, no choking smoke. We don't know that our soul is refreshed and renewed each infinitesimal dot of time, and there's no waiting for the love to come, and there's no distance for love to cover, and there's no cost for love to grant its blessings.

Yes, we eternally are. Our souls, yours, and mine, are one — squeezed in the seed of a feeling which sprouts and fills the timeless and dimensionless vastness of the most purely conceptual existence.

You don't need to miss me,

my love.

We are.

Do not melt, my dear one. If you choose to fade, then my world will lose the moon, the stars, the sun, and everything that makes this universe worth existing because my universe and its beauty are YOU. Now, when you have put before my eyes the painting which is of yours and my love, I ask, or perhaps request, to take a break from writing and let us hear from each other in real. I want to sit opposite you and hear you. I want to witness these beautiful words that you write, curling and tossing and flowing from those lips that I so wish to kiss. Let me, oh let me travel to you and see you before my heart loses its mind. Yes, it is the heart, which is my mind and my dictator. What life is which is lived without listening to one's heart?

I urge you to listen to your heart and grant its wish of seeing me. I know and I realize that the days ahead of us are uncertain, and the path lying before us is unclear, but can we allow our souls to burn and vanish in the desire to see the love that is real? Oh my treasure, my beloved, life is too short to be wasted in not seeing the one who is by all means the partner of our souls. You, in every way, complete me; then why must I live miles away from you?

Traveling to your part of the world will just take a flying ticket. You do not have to worry about showing me your beautiful city. All the monuments, the history, and the beauty of your place are too small compared to what your presence will bring to me. To talk of sins, we are not destructive. The sea, the forests, the wildlife, and humans are not being hurt by us. We are just star-crossed lovers who are just here on this planet to experience love and to depart on the note that love, only love, can save this world.

Maybe, there is no tomorrow for us. Perhaps, if we depart (oh, how much ache this word brings!), then we should not carry a wound of not ever seeing each other. The other day, I was looking at the rising sun. Because these are the days I am an insomniac, probably love-struck, so I saw a giant beautiful ball rising like a fresh orange in the sky and then the sky was no more sky but a humongous canvas which was painted by the Unseen. That moment I asked myself how many days will I live to see that beauty. The days when I can't bear the insomnia then I must take refuge in sleeping pills, won't they take the right from me to witness that beauty?

Now, my darling, you are more than a beautiful sunrise or the sparkling stars. So allow me to witness your charm, your magical existence before I lose all rights on this life, this beautiful world, and you. I fear life is slipping away, and so are you. I don't remember when was the last time that God gave me someone that stayed with me forever and who is still mine. I have faith in God, but – somewhere the broken heart, rusted wounds echo, 'Oh, girl! Love him, before he is gone. Before you lose every reason for your existence.'

My love, we are nomads. We are traveling in parallel universes, and there is uncertainty hanging around my neck. I know our meeting would bring a desire for more, but isn't it better to have little than to have none ever? Let me hear you. Let me say these words to you while looking into your eyes. We don't need dinner or lunch but just freshly brewed coffee and a quiet afternoon. Is that too much to ask for?

My mind has lost to the heart. Either I have you in this life or not, I will always be yours. Find yourself in warm arms of mine. Yours. (When someone writes 'yours,' they make the strongest commitment, and I make this promise with all my heart, soul, and mind.) So yes,

Yours,

Only yours.

For that roaming dot in the sky, on which all the light around seems to coalesce, as if to burn everything else or rather as if to bear witness that everything is light, and colors are just a dull disguise!

For any revelation suddenly typed on a page, which all the words before couldn't let see, whose deliverance soaks and coats any other following word on any following page, like colored spectacles which change your vision so wonderfully and consistently that you do not wish to remove them anymore!

For any outbreak of jubilee in a sleepy morning, with sonorous laughter veined by sighs as remnants of a last night of many spent in veiling and praying, accruing offers, oaths, propositions at the blessed feet of the Holy, beyond any possible hope, before the impossible broke in the tissue of reality, to make everyone doubt about the very sense and existence of that denial –– the oxymoron denying word 'impossible' is!

Oh, the effects your sudden words had on me! You and I... meeting?! I sipped and savored all of your words, and I imagined myself seeing what you were painting with them. But I must confess that I was rendered incapacitated to fully focus on them, for here, by my side, I already daydreamed I was feeling your warmth, your fragrance, your subtle sounds.

Truly, we could enclose ourselves in a box, faking the world like in that curious story in a toon for children, or even less, we could seclude ourselves apart from the colorful world in a box with harsh steel walls, for those unadorned surfaces would disappear anyway from the acknowledgment of our consciousness, replaced by unclosed and unclosing, limitless, liberating spaces of sidereal magnitude... as nothing else would matter but our reciprocal presence, nothing else would be more powerful than that shrinking to zero of an unbearable distance, as if our closeness was the prodigious artifact capable of liberating the whole Creation from any limitation, barrier, captivity, forbidding and banning.

Yet, I have to say, how much I would love to have your eyes consider glimpses of the seamless sequence of neighborhoods (in a mathematical sense) of the world I determined by living, and which in turn determined me, for I still am, in part, the outcome of the inputs and feedbacks of whatever has been surrounding, touching, and pushing me.

Because you wouldn't just witness a smoking dish, the façade of a church, the loud sound of a crowd reverberating fragments of a language which is foreign to your tender ears. I daydream of gently biting and suckling until my own oneiric construction almost pushes me down the precipice of love madness, but you – as I was saying – would also experience my interaction with all this, you would see it through my eyes just like, right now, I'm experiencing that sun in the sky through yours, and you would know me even more... you would live the world a second time, through me, and the Creation would become a pair of spectacles you could wear to observe and know me a little more.

But I was saying, I started reading everything you describe in your letter as if we were observing it together, and at some point, I imagined me seeing myself and listening to myself, and I started evaluating myself... but through your eyes... and I wondered, what will you think of what you'll see and hear, and what will you feel about it all... and I started panicking.

No, not that I think that your judgment would be harsh,

cruel, or unfair. I know it wouldn't... I know it won't! Because in the scope of your descriptions, there wasn't only me, scrutinized through discovering lenses, but you, as well, and this had to make me reflect that you probably share the same fears of mine, "will I be enough, for her/him? Will she/he love me anyway, despite my imperfect nature, when my passionate words won't be able to hide it anymore?"

Oh, this abysmal distance! Our words dare to cross back and forth with gargantuan steps and jumps... a distance that tears us apart little by little, whenever we wish to lose ourselves in each other's embrace. Yet, a distance that protects us somehow from the risks brought by confronting ourselves and each other into that challenge being two, like two irregular tiles of a puzzle in desperate need to be matched.

But those two puzzles can't make complete sense, on their own, isn't it? The picture they reveal together can't be immolated on the altar of the deity of the selfish comfort. Don't you agree?

Oh, my dear, the specters you evoke in some of your lines. Why, those words about the end? Why now, just now that we speak about meeting, as if it was a new beginning? Is our distance in space replicated into a length in time, allowing us to make this bond last as long as there's breath and blood? Would our closeness in the tridimensional universe suddenly transfer itself like a deceiving Trojan horse, into the temporal landscape, pushing the beginning and the end, crash one against the other, making them disintegrate, and shattering us along, with them? Are we fated to this distance in such a way that to dare to break it would necessarily destroy us?!

But, now look! Look at what I'm doing here and now,

engulfed and deceived by those ghosts I breed and nurture with my own mind! If it's our feeling, that powerful feeling we share, and which shades us both with the same indescribable hue of craving, and which pushes us to desire to be the closest as if we were the bleeding, torn halves of the same pulsating heart. If it's our feeling, which is of suffering as long as we're far away from each other, which will only be of the most pure and fulfilled joy, as soon as we will be together, reunited on the same tiny plot of soil, under the same handful of sparkling photons that traveled just for us, and only for us, to bless us, from one hundred and forty-nine million kilometers, premised all this, why should I fear anything, especially the end, from the most happiest circumstance my mind can, and wishes to, think about right now: that is you and I cocooning each other tight, like quarks in a proton since before the dawn of time?

I'll be ticking off the days from my calendar with increasing frenzy till that day we'll meet will come.

Yours, only yours (as you wisely teach me).

Shhhh…. Hush!! I wish I could put my fingers on your lips and say, "Ssshh!! Don't panic. Don't be worried. Aren't I enough for you? I believe I am, so how can you, whose presence can make my hot summer day beautiful like a spring afternoon, think would not be enough?"

I don't care if I do not get to see great monuments of your city. I don't care if your city doesn't sleep and its air echoes with horns of moving vehicles. All I care is to see you: for once and for all. I want to reduce all the numbers to 0.000000 and infinity. I want to breathe among the same atoms as you do. I want the sound to touch our ears together. My love, just as love is immeasurable, so must be our souls and bodies.

What started with soul is becoming mortal now, and it is scary, but at the same time it brings to me an infinite anxiety and joy. Shall I bring with me my favourite Rumi and read to you? Or do you think, we would never get time to talk of great poets? Whatever is to happen, let it be the breathtaking moment of our lives. I think, let the time paint our day and we must be silent till then. Oh no, by silence I do not mean not writing. Do write me till I come. It is your writing that gives me every reason to wake up every morning with a hope.

I forgot to even start the letter with 'Dear' because as soon as I got it— but first I must tell how your letter came to me unexpectedly. I didn't expect such a quick reply. I thought you would take a week to write back and it will take another seven days to reach me. However, in the morning, I made myself a coffee, decided to have it in my garden, but as soon as I opened the door, I saw a familiar envelope peeping out from the postbox. I kept my coffee on the ground, since my brain stopped working for a moment, and ran towards the postbox, picked up the mail and came back to where I left my coffee. I sat on the floor, tore the envelope and started to read. I couldn't control my tears. Happy tears, I must say. To know that soon the stars, the moon and the sun will be seen by us from the same lens is a thought worth living for.

Thus not to delay our long-awaited meetup, I have already started to make arrangements for my travel. As soon as I get a visa and ticket, I will be there. In your arms? I don't know. I wonder if I will immediately run to you and hold you, or I will gasp and be lost in the moment. Be patient, another half of your heart is coming to complete you.

Yours. Always.

Oh, you. And, ah, me. I can understand that oscillating state between suspension and agitation you must have fallen prey to, even though it comes from within your sidereal soul, because it's the same way I'm living since you announced to me your intention to resolve this problem which looked unsolvable.

There are experiences in life, we learn to know by accruing around a hard and rough kernel of rules which seem to be able to challenge the eons ahead and all of the mutations and permutations they carry along with themselves. And we get so used to such rules that never would we ever consider the possibility to defy them, and even less to change them.

This distance we share, just like crowds of other lovers share a bone-melting closeness, is like oil thrown on a fire of desire which only gets fed to grow up to humongous dimensions. This distance we share, which in its own weird way is our closeness-to-be, has been with us and between us, and around us, and within us as well, as if it was a founding and indispensable component of our precious alchemy. For so long, it seems to me it is as ancient as the pyramids sprayed with sand and wonder, as antique as the bones of the giant beasts which once roamed the world under the pleased stare of God, as primigenial as the celestial bodies sluggishly rolling round and round on the invisible planes of the most admirable space perfections. It seems to me that like everything fated, or doomed to last, it should and it must, it has to be given a precise, everlasting, defining law in which you and I would obviously be the singular and notable constants and every other term would revolve around us and explain why, oh why! we can't be closer.

But now you, oh you, you summon the power of your freedom to choose. And you invert the adamant pillars of the whole universe with such power, and in this way you are going to break – no, you already broke – those forces which have been keeping us apart, thus demonstrating how strong your power of choice to bind us and wrap us with the same cocoon of intertwined limbs and lips and love is, even stronger than that which keeps an atom together and the above-lying matter too.

I start reading a newspaper, but I put it down, for I'm sure I heard the doorbell ring. But no, not really. I start sipping chamomile tea, but I abandon it somewhere, just like your coffee plagued by the same fate, to stay there, like an unperturbed little pond, forgotten, and cool down like water stained by a playful kid, all this because I heard the doorbell ring, and I had to go check, no matter if it's past midnight. But no, not really. It wasn't ringing.

I start writing and... really, can fiction be more interesting than this reality awaiting ahead? Can even only its hypothetical description surpass it? Oh, come on. I do everything I can but nothing is able to have a hold on me anymore because only daydreaming can save me from this wait, which is at once torment and bliss. So I daydream, again and again, and I know you can believe me when I say it sometimes eases things, and sometimes makes them even more complicated.

But see, as you said (or rather implied), there won't be any door ringing, to begin with, for I'll get you at the airport and... Okay. I think I hear an airplane landing, its humongous engines filling the air with their roar... Now, who said only Sunday's bells can ring when the heart gets lost in an embrace with its other half? The loudly roaring engines of an airplane seem perfectly fitting as well. Come soon, please. Love.

P.S. Bring Rumi, Poe, King, Shakespeare, and Austen, whoever you wish.

But please, warn them, that we might even end up spending hours talking about nothing with the apex of our delight, without feeling the need to involve them in the conversation... and without feeling the slightest sense of guilt about that.

So they may be conscious of the risk.

My dear Mine, You would be thinking, "What a senseless way to begin a letter." But my beloved, love takes away all the senses. It makes us forget that humans cannot be possessed, and this one word, 'mine,' is such a great thing to say. This very word can take away the heart and can break it in seconds. Well, I better leave this profound discussion for some other time because now I have news for you. Indeed, good news and bad news. What shall I start with? Well, I know your heart is beating fast, your hands are shivering, so I must not tease you more. The good news is... you start counting the sunsets and sunrises... When the moon will be full, the heart will be empty, and eyes will be dry, you will find me in your arms. How many sunsets should you cross from the calendar of love and longing? Well, seven. Yes, seven more days, and I will get on the iron bird, beg the weather to stay calm, and fly to you (I wish I could add here 'for eternity'). I have packed, unpacked, and packed my bag a zillion times. Seeing nothing apart from black, white, and blue in my wardrobe, I went to buy some colors. I bought pink. I kept the dress in a bag and then thought to myself what a silly choice. I went back to the store, chose the red one, and went to the salesgirl and asked her for an exchange without exchanging looks. She was cold. Looked devastated as if she had cried all night. I silently made a prayer for her. It's strange that I have started to believe my prayers get accepted since I have got my visa and tickets. Well, I came home and then regretted buying such a bold color. I know I am overthinking, but I have my own fears. Fear of not being able to stop the world around you when I am there right in front of your eyes. Apart from flowers, air, clouds, sun, and us, I want everything to stop. I want Magritte to look from the sky and think to repaint his 'The Lovers' without preventing the intimacy between two lovers. I want to dance with you to happy tunes on the streets. I will bring the audio cassettes with all the music I always wanted to listen to with you. Yes, along with Rumi, Whitman, Joyce, and all that can take our souls away. But again, will we get time from creating our own verses and reading what is already written? I panic, so I walk around. I lie down and hear my heart exploding. What is it? Was my soul always incomplete, and now it has found that its other half lives miles away, so it is restless and desperate to be completed? This takes me to the bad news. And the bad news is, this anxiety might take my life, and you would have to live your rest of life without ever seeing me. Well, well. Before you lose your mind and tear this off for such cruel humor. As I said, I have lost my senses.

Yours.

P.S:

I don't want you to come to the airport because I will probably faint or cry. There are various worse possibilities. I will be a little unkind and leave you without any information on my flight. DO forgive me. Just this time. You have to; what other choice do you have, no?

Oh, my beloved! I love you, and I now live in a countdown, that before your next coming, which I can't and I don't want to stop, as much as I couldn't and didn't want to stop that I previously lived, that since when you announced me the day of your long-sought arrival. Come soon, again! Soon, I implore you! Grind the mountains! Make the deserts blossom! Flood with empathy the drought in the aridity of the hearts of men... but come soon, I beg you on my scorched knees! I have never hated our distance more than No. I cannot let such words stain these pages, now. Not AFTER YOU. What was I telling you, in my last, or perhaps last but one letter, about lapses of time and their extremes? I can't even recall it right now, as scattered as I am in the past before we finally met (a never-ending, dull time, that before, I have to say), in this present of confusion in which time and existence are fragmented and suspended between the bliss of the memories and the ache of missing you. And in all the precious lapse between, in those billions and billions notable and valuable moments we were able centrifugally squeeze in between, in each one of which I am and exist and rejoice to the point of fainting (let's not lose our sense together, you and I, but rather let's take turns so to be able to hold and keep each other from falling down and breaking down to little crumbs of bone, flesh, and soul). How can I know where and when and what I live, if where I am and when I am and what I see and what I do fade, more often than not, in where we have been... were... have been... are! I don't know!!! I don't know anymore and I don't want to know!!!... And when we were and in what we saw and what we did. You! It must have been your light, which radiates beyond the bodily senses, which first coats and then soaks through the thoughts and the heart-beats with a dress of felicity reaching the core of the heart, to the depth of the soul, and it stays stuck there to sing in silence because the output senses merrily abide to a lethargic numbness for they can't possibly convey and express all that blitheness without disrupting the body in its fundamental components so to let them free to wildly dance as if they weren't just bricks to serve and compose, but rather baroque palaces which shine by themselves. It must have been your light, I was saying before getting lost in my praise for you, to have imprinted itself, not just in my retinas to flash your eyes and your smiles, but in my neurons too, to draw and redraw the maps of our mindless routes we ventured knowing only that we were together and everything else was inconsequential; and in both my malleus and eardrum, to reconstruct your words of love like divine promises and the fluted sound of your voice; and in the furrows and ridges of my labyrinthine epidermis like bursts of the warmth of your silken skin; and in the cavities of my nostrils which at times refuse to let more vital air pass through for to prevent the smell of your skin from getting slowly worn off. And on the tormented surface of my lips, which my teeth incessantly assault to replace with the pain of their pulp, the way worse unquenchable craving of your lips, of your skin, and of your taste. Tell me how, even the seven wonders that this troubled humanity has been building, losing, and then regretting and daydreaming about since the dawn of creativity, could appear to me any more than the most uninteresting speckles of unworthy dust, even if they were right before me, when I had so many lapis lazuli and emerald and rubies embedded in the girdle of time you and I made out of blissful love in the time we shared together! Oh, the pink of that other dress, as if all the petals from all the flowers of all the peach trees had willingly and joyfully sacrificed themselves and chosen to fall to dress you and your soul, tenderness on tenderness, simplicity on simplicity, finesse on finesse! Ah, that bold burgundy of your dress is the Red Sea crashing on and slaying the pharaoh leading the armies of my dark days, dawn of an eternal summer of a voluptuous abundance of ripened, juicy fruits falling on my lap and in my hands as if the winter already forgotten had carefully carved on their crevices my name! And, those blacks and those whites in your other clothes, sometimes alone and sometimes combined! Together, to witness your simplicity and at once, your sharp and focused vision on how things are, and should be: chromatic statements, imbued with your personality, which I can't but adore! And separated, like two extremes set apart to underline and enhance their mutual need for each other. The whites, to suggest the openness like that of a blank page of the times we were, and still are, writing, independently and even more together. To remind of the sum of all the colors reunited in a cheerful symposium to signify that we were living. It was the sum of all the experiences and the hopes and the dreams, finally coalesced in the most striking perfection of a dream turned into reality. And that black, sucking in all the reality of the universe around, just like you were sucking my perception, and all of my acknowledgment, as if you had in you, at once, all that which exists. The singular and unique entity where all that which exists dips the tips of its toes, and the hole in which I would have loved to take a plunge and sink down, down, down,

down, down, down, down. Seven times. To find your seven ways to be perfect the way you are, to understand those seven complements which can fix and fulfill my seven ways to be imperfect, to discover the seven reasons for which to live in your heart, in your mind, in your soul, would be better than living here on this ball of mud; or flying over the masses of pilgrims who roam miles with fatigue and pray on countless fatigues for their belief makes it all possible; or swimming among the massive creatures which had left the seas and took millions years, by tasting their own salty tears cried at the apex of the darkness, to understand they had been missing them all the time; or sitting in the lotus position in the most magnificent quartz temple to an unknown deity erected by forgotten hands in an underground cave on Mars; or just existing, eternally suspended. The eyes look for boundaries that don't exist anymore, perhaps because they never existed, to begin with, in the gargantuan gaseous giants known as Pillars of the Universe supporting the weight of the meaning we give to the word "commotion", or in the heart of the Himalayas, right at its center, as a minuscule speckle of marble that should have never gained any consciousness of itself for its matched with the acknowledgment of all the billions of tons of rock around crushing on it and holding it eternally at its place, till its carbonate heart won't implode for the pain, till the earth won't explode setting it free, that little tiny heart of the Himalayas nobody ever knew about! Should I keep telling you of all the places where I rather would NOT be, if I can be with you? But it isn't only yours, that vision which insists in trying and trying to dethrone the reality around me, as if it wanted to be crowned as the actual reality, as if this could supersede and replace the current circumstances and bring you back. "Only" and "yours", together... what a silly monstrosity! I am experiencing an amazing phenomenon these days, which only and irrefutably, I summon as witness on our good side at the heavenly court to testify and certify that our meeting was wanted, conjured, disposed and decreed by that highest court itself! Because I sometimes have memories of us, of that precious time like endless laces of beads of jubilation, not only from my own perspective, but from above, as if my soul, for the elation, had been like a kite quickly ascending above, beyond any gravity, and from there it had watched us. Our little plummeted heads, immersed in the crowd of this eager humanity, flowing like a river in the dusty roads we dig by going on. And our heads waving back and forth, left and right, at the unison of a music no one but us could hear. Our hands intertwined together to compose a tissue no one can tear apart. Our lips letting the soul in our breaths embrace each other in the delirium of the most complete fulfillment. And us, like I was saying, getting smaller and smaller with the crowd, with the continent, with the planet, with the solar system, with the galaxy, from the teary and laughing eyes of my soul flying to God, at once, propelled by your love, observing that point becoming smaller and smaller, till it seems it isn't there anymore, but it rather is there, for there is happiness, and nothing could count more.

Amen.

Now that I am back, I feel like I have lost something. I don't know why I took so long to write after reaching. What was keeping me away from writing? Emptiness? Completeness? I unpacked my bags and broke into tiny pieces because everything smells of you. I want to get rid of everything that brings you here but I actually don't want to. Oh! Oh Heavens! What am I writing? What am I thinking? I keep wondering why you didn't hide my passport and threw my tickets away so I would have never returned. I am sorry I didn't allow you to come to the airport. The tears in public do nothing but bring unnecessary attention. I wonder would I have only shed tears or lost my soul too were you at the airport. When I arrived, I thought you would write me a letter telling how much you miss me. But then a week passed by and I took the initiative. Here I am blank and empty. Did I leave anything behind? I know I left my red dress there. I left it intentionally. I left it so you don't forget me, but I think what our souls and bodies discovered would never let us forget each other. How do they talk of lovers seeing stars and waves together in romantic novels? We never worried about the sky or the moon. All we had to see and drown in was each other's presence. Now that I am back, I'm certain that I can never make there again nor you will ever come here. I ask myself, how I will ever live without you. Every morning I wake up imagining you are here, holding me in your arms. But dreams take seconds to fade. Can I keep writing or go far away? When you look at your palm, does it remind you of me? Before parting, I wrote my name there. You kept asking why I was tickling you. I wasn't. I was writing mine and your name. It's hard to move on— Look, the milk is boiled. I need to fix the breakfast for me and him. I need to see the psychiatrist today. I... I have to come back to what I call 'Silent Chamber'. Nothing moves here except the needles of the clock. I need to restart the masquerade and pretend as if the absence of love causes no harm. I have to pretend life is a blessing until happiness comes over for coffee and decides to stay in my chamber. Will she love you like I do? Will we meet again? Can we break the rules? Oh, the phone is ringing, and your lips are burning on my wrist. I am shrinking, I think. Perhaps, the circumference around me is shrinking, and I am afraid it will crush me.

Take me home.

Oh! We are homeless, aren't we?

Yours

(or not)

It took me days, my love, to... Yes, I called you mine. It's to reaffirm, even in fleeting, fading, vaporous words, a concept which is so deeply embedded in me that even only the contemplation of a different possibility has left my mind still feeling like dangling between the ages, and the stages, of the two of us.

The same effect of the cage of that majestic bird living in the humid penumbra of the Amazonian forest which was said to have never left the branched safety of its tree, and when was forced to leave, for the tree was cut by steel teeth and heartless hands pushing mindless levers, the poor bird flew to the moon in the desperate wish to find a home nobody could ever pull down... or perhaps that is just the way we want to look at it, and the poor bird just left to die above the clouds, where there are no trees, and there's no home for birds, but only for souls.

But nobody wants to admit it because it's too desolating for the heart, too shattering for the mind, too estranging for the spirit, to think that his home was destroyed so carelessly, or that he couldn't think of wanting to try to find another home, before choosing to want no life, if just that home was torn off of its own. I feel guilty.

Reading your words... ah, my dear, that confession, that you had been awaiting my letter, right after you left... the implied statement of your delusion... it's heart-breaking! To think that I wrote it, indeed! Haven't you gotten it?! It's so tragic if the world surrounding us conjures against us, preventing our words from reaching each other, like it would rather be supposed to do, after having conjured not only to make us know each other, not only to make us fall for each other, and finally even to have made us meet, and be like one.

But you had to leave, yes, and I admit that this could even make one despair and think the world doesn't want us to fulfill this most beautiful dream. As if the trees, the rivers, the mountains, even the stars above, had all turned their back to us and decided to let us go astray towards a destiny of distance and delusions, towards a fate of fear and frustration. It's hard, it's terribly hard, right now!

And we knew it, before meeting, we knew it well, what would have followed would have been worse than any distance before... because how can losing be not infinitely worse than craving? But tell me why we met, then! Why? Because our souls, stills of infinity dripping in the veins of these fragile existences lasting an ache, or a laughter, knew that no past or future could have any significance, before the power and the freedom in our choice to give ourselves a chance to give birth to a dream into a statement for our souls, hearts, minds, and bodies to write in the invisible scroll of subsistence.

We have been one, my dearest being in the universe, and this has changed the balances of the cosmos forever, and nothing has been the same since then. God Himself looks back at the vast prairies and oceans of all the dimensions and the worlds He wisely and masterfully created. And whenever His omniscience sweeps this universe, this age and these days, He witnesses the statement which our love penned... and how could He not smile, tell me, if He planned it since before you and I saw the sky and reflected on its immensity?

God is blessing us, from His painless Heaven which secretly pervades all of the cosmic dust, for our love we share is

His gift for us. I see all the signs, especially, paradoxically, in all the challenges it has been pushing us to face all this time: the distance, the walls, the assaults made of our own "it can't" and "it won't" of that discouragement which has been sieging, in all evidence for it is envious of what our hearts know, in their depth: that "it can" and "it will", if only we can be brave enough.

If only, I have to remind myself, in first place, in these times after us in which I willingly get lost in my own mind. If only, as I was saying, we lean on each other, and take turn to be fulcrum and lever for each other, to push each other further, to pull each other in and out, anywhere we mutually decide to go, helping each other, and welcoming each other's help, for I don't know how love should be otherwise. Tell me, if all the troubles we've been going through, haven't been, for our love, and for each one of us, like the sepulchral chrysalis for the wondrous butterfly pushing and pulling to conquer its narrow path to the light!

We must look beyond them! They've been forging us, like fire on steel, to make us stronger in our determination! And tell me, have there been only challenges? I found it, your beautiful red dress, for when I read about it I immediately turned my home upside down, revolutionizing its geology and geography, till I found it! Oh, you! How could the present struggles of craving you, thousands and millions and billions times more than before, now that I know the aroma of your skin, now that I know the symphony of your voice, now that I know the mind-deranging pleasure of sinking in the tender consistence and existence of your flesh, be stronger than the absolute, undeniable, incontrovertible reality, as true as the ocean, of our meeting, of our union, this beautiful dress of yours, as red as the boiling, roaring blood in our veins, is a testimony of?

This is reality. And we made it happen, despite what seemed meant to be, perhaps because that, attracting each other like the most powerful magnets in existence that, is what is really meant to be. Look, at your beautiful soul which knows no boundaries. Look at how it pushed you to sign my palm with your name. I am your property. You have the most complete dominium of me, and I couldn't and wouldn't ask any other owner than you. I am yours, yours, and yours forever.

P.S. We made it happen, please, remember. And we will again, somehow, beyond everything else. Because it's in us, such immense power. Look within, you know it's there! I love you.

I have no answers to 'whys,' but I do know that now if one day I wake up to news of you becoming a better half of someone else, I might not live a day over that news.

I was on a train this afternoon and couldn't help listening to two girls talking of their love lives. It seemed to me life isn't easier for anyone. The more one builds up the castle of perfection, the less they find love.

We are undeniably the halves of one soul. It's only time that has decided to keep us apart. I have loved you in every way and in every form of love I was aware of. I couldn't make love strong enough to reduce these distances and make us one. I couldn't give you courage to steal me from the world, but the time has come.

My love, I write here with my melancholic heart, I am leaving. I am going to start a journey to places that won't allow me to look back. Do not think I am leaving you here. I am carrying you inside my heart. I am aware of the magnets that will keep us together. If I stay here, I won't be able to survive another day.

I am glad you have my red dress. I hope it survives till you overcome this pain. I am well informed of the pain which can be brought in by the unexpected departure of a loved one. Do I have any option? Can I make the universe change our lives? How shall I be reborn and claim you mine? How can I knock these walls down which define us —— religion, color, nationalities?

Truth is, I can only love you. I cannot bring revolution and change what hasn't been changed for centuries. To say that you belong to me is all I can ever ask for. You have completed me and it is time for me to carry you in my heart and move to a heaven which no one has seen.

Thank you for giving me a place in your heart and making me certain that one cannot be homeless as long as they are residing in someone's heart. Thank you for restoring my faith in humans; all my life I believed only animals are capable of loving.

I am here, wrapping my arms around you, looking into your eyes and taking you back on a day when I held you for the last time. Remember what I said? So you must wait for God to unite us. Who knows our paths cross again, or perhaps I will be waiting for you there and run with you into the stars and live there for eternity.

Forgive me for not staying long enough, but I hope you do understand that I deserve peace. I deserve rest. Life has been a terrific journey. I am glad on this rough road I had a few days of love, joy, and serenity; I had a few hours to love and live.

My dear one, I am sending you my black journal, my photograph, and your shirt which you wore the day we met. It helped me to live in your fragrance as if you were right here.

Did I ever tell you I didn't sleep the night I was with you because it was so hard to move my eyes away from the light illuminating from heaven in my arms? I kept looking at you until dawn and kissed your face.

I am at peace now. I hope you find someone who loves you, cherishes you, and protects you. I hope I loved you enough. I hope I loved you more than you have ever been loved.

With a kiss on your lips, I close my final letter.

With the madness of love and beyond,

Yours and always yours,

Everything.

Undelivered Letter

All the bile in the liver isn't bitter than me now. All the minuscule fragments of a glass abandoned at falling aren't as shattered as me now. Oh, there's no perfect castle on this earth; and hearts as scorched as they are by the absurd amounts of pain we senselessly pour and throw onto each other... but this is why, this is why! we need love: to fill and mend and render bearable, if not irrelevant, all of the imperfections!

I have read your letter one thousand times, each time hoping there might be a different conclusion to be traced and reconstructed and drawn, from your words and lines and paragraphs; and especially between them, each time ending dying on each disconsolate statement, like hit by a hand materializing from the page like wicked sorcery and stabbing me with a dagger sparkling with polished gemstones getting scattered with squirts of my own blood.

But I cannot find a different conclusion, in your words, other than that which is way too evident. You are leaving. You are leaving me, even if I understand you believe you are not, and I believe you when you say you will keep me in your heart, for how could I not believe that? For you are not really leaving me... you are rather abandoning us, you are breaking us apart and... "I couldn't make love strong enough to reduce these distances and make us one."

My mind is feverish, an aching, pulsating, punching entanglement of ifs and whys and no-s and perhaps... and some lines of your letter, like this one, are no less than fanged monsters surfacing again and again from the restless oceanic surface of that shattered and quaked mass my mind currently is, monsters angry and hungry for different answers you won't give, of a present alternative to what you decreed in what now feels like a cruelly immutable past.

Was it you, or me, or anyone, who had the responsibility to make our love strong enough to make us push the mountains and reduce the oceans to puddles even a kid would effortlessly hop over? Or wasn't our love rather supposed to be strong enough to push us to make a change? "I couldn't give you courage to steal me from the world."

This has shattered me. Seriously, my blood has seeped throughout my pores, abandoning me, choosing to evaporate so to leave this ground on which I'm left crawling; so to leave me, and disown me, for it wasn't for this shameful outcome, that it kept confidently circulating in me again and again all this time!

For if you couldn't give me that courage to steal you from the world... or, rather, I could correct you... for yes, I couldn't steal you, but from your world. From yours, sadly, not from mine. But no, the pain and the anger is messing up with my logical capabilities! It's neither from yours, nor from mine, but rather from their juxtaposition.

For this is the foolishness of men, that which makes them look at our societies, and proclaim that this and that are no less than two different worlds, separate, irreconcilable, all for reasons which are in their heads, and in their hearts, in what they think and believe; as if that was stronger than the banal, yet universal truth that we all have a beating heart, and two eyes and two ears and a nose and a mouth and four limbs and this is the only thing which can be stated for sure, out of any belief. And so, tell me, in what way we ever differ, after all!

So there is just one world, to which we both belong, and

there shouldn't be any need to talk about stealing. As if you were a helpless property of your own world when it's rather that the world is ours, or at least it should, if they only stopped hammering their flags in the ground, and worse, in the hearts and in the lives of others, thinking they can own it all.

But this doesn't help me: being right, doesn't help me, or you, or us. So it's twice, or thrice! The sense of guilt I feel. For having not grown enough courage to overflow the shaking dams of my limits and boundaries, and bring you away from your own, like a joyful flood. For the way it must feel for you, leaving me without wanting it... Tell me, do you consider me responsible? Should I have done more?! Why do I ask, it's so clear you think so... I feel so guilty, that these apneas I'm going through since I received your letter could even be a sign, not only of my pain, but also of the proposition of my body to sink itself, and of my life to leave me, just for I culpably couldn't collect enough courage to pull down all the walls for you!

But I also feel guilty, for your decision, for I wasn't able to let you see that there was hope, in this love we share(d), even more for it was so hard to keep nurturing it. That "just", the existence of such a feeling we had sanctified with those few, precious, unforgettable days together, was such a power-ful reality which deserved to be protected, preserved, and defended, despite all the difficulties!

How tragic! How grotesque! That what I thought could be an event able to cement our sentiment, and make it stronger, rather turned out being its unexpected finishing blow! I know, I know, it's not in those heavenly and blessed days of two persons just being themselves, singularly and together, enshrining in soul and body what in all evidence was a shared feelings no other than God must have blessed their hearts and life with... but I felt and still feel ready to resist and wait, sustained and pervaded by all the strength the concrete realization, even only for a few days, of our dream, resist and wait for us, for you and me... and now I discover that the same event, or rather what necessarily followed, an even more painful separation and an even less bearable distance, has rendered useless my resistance, and ridiculous that patience I was and still am wishing to nurture, when you expected me to steal you and I rather failed and deluded you, when you don't feel like fighting anymore for your feelings, for mine, for us...

And now, tell me, how can I fight against your will, which I consider worthy of the maximum respect, even when it hurts us, and you and me, even when it turns out being the least expected menace, from within, for our bond? I am writing and writing and... I think it would be useless, or that it would just hurt you more, and me too, when your answer, whose content I could not be able to foresee as much as I couldn't see this epoch. making one come, had to reach me and hit me... For you don't need words from me. You need facts. You need statements written in the pages of life, and not on a page of paper which can be ripped while shouting, soaked with tears, or burnt in the fire.

You need to leave your home one day, unaware because a lack of answers from me will have made you think that I agreed with you on ending our bond. You need to leave one morning, to take care of your day as usual, and find me sitting at your door, with all of my miseries you have been able to love and praise as if they were blessings, but also with a new light in my eyes; the light which only those who have finally broken, or even climbed the barriers of their own limits which once looked tall to the clouds and reached above and beyond, to discover to be way more than what they thought was possible.

You need to see me sitting at your door, waiting for you, craving for you, and doing everything for you –– in spite of this world which foolishly pretends to be divided and in this way only denies itself, to believe with me that each and every distance can be surpassed. If only we stop believing the lie that this can't happen and that can't be done, if only we acknowledge and admit that it's solely in our hands, and how much we are ready to sacrifice of the world they try to impose on us, to conquer together the world that only exists in which we are free to love each other, for not even God thinks of denying the feeling bridging our hearts, the one He rather blesses.

And, that day, that pretty day with a sky hued with a blue like it was never seen since Adam named the Moon, you will believe again, that we can be more than a quickly vanishing oasis of Heaven in an everlasting Hell... that we can be, forever.

You will believe again in all this, that day.

You will believe in us, again.

As long as there's life to thank God for.

About River

Once upon a time, there was a glacier who had been standing the passage of the seasons.

But then a fiercely Sun of passion began to sing his songs, and the ice couldn't but melt away.

And water feel through the cracks of the mountain, down to her most remote depths, into her silent, pitch black womb.

And there the water grew, and grew more and more, drop after drop, amongst calcareous towers, pillars and fangs, till it couldn't be still or just plick plock pluck anymore, till the nostalgia of the memories of the air was too much to bear.

So it started gnawing the stone until it found more cracks downwards, and there it fled through.

Filling its liquidity with photons and freshness, it started jumping and dancing, laughing and singing, for it just had had another proof of the most groundbreaking of the Laws.

And if you go and see for yourself, you'll still witness it all by yourself: the river on its way, at once always the same and always different, perennially immutable at its core and yet forever mutable on the surface.

And not even its destination will be the final one, for once again the mighty sun, embued with the Light of Love, will build, for its vaporous feet, unseen stairs climbing to the clouds, and the rain will fall with pain and the ice will feed on that, but nothing is ever really lost.

For "end" is just the root of "endless".

Somewhere on this planet (the only one we got),
2024

About Huma

I am Huma, a hopeless romantic whose journey through life has been as unpredictable as it is passionate. By day, I serve as the Learning and Development Head, but beyond my professional persona, I find solace in reading and writing. My heart is captivated by a love for travel, a pursuit that once led me to Kafka's grave. It was his "Letters to Milena" that inspired the seed for this book.

In 2018, I connected with River, and together, we embarked on the ambitious journey of bringing this book to life. These letters are an expression of my love for all the people I have ever loved and lost, for those who share my life now, and for the love I have yet to embrace.

Dear readers, may these letters resonate with your own experiences of love and loss, and may they inspire you to cherish every moment with those you hold dear. Thank you for joining me on this heartfelt journey.